BATMAN™
FOREVER

Adapted by Andrew Helfer
Based on a screenplay written by
Lee Batchler & Janet Scott Batchler and Akiva Goldsman

A GOLDEN BOOK • NEW YORK
Western Publishing Company, Inc., Racine, Wisconsin 53404

Batman was the greatest crime fighter in Gotham City. Whenever criminals tried to break the law, Batman was there to stop them. When they launched a crime spree, Batman would swoop out of the sky on his Batrope or roar down the street in his Batmobile–just in the nick of time!

Two-Face was one of the criminals Batman had not caught—yet! Two-Face and his gang committed crimes all over Gotham City. They worked so quickly, no one could keep up with them. Batman was only one man. To stop Two-Face, he would need help.

When he wasn't fighting crime, Batman had a secret identity. He was Bruce Wayne, the wealthiest man in Gotham City.

Bruce often helped people. One day he met a young circus acrobat named Dick Grayson. Dick was an orphan and needed a place to live. Bruce invited Dick to stay in Wayne Manor.

Dick liked living in the mansion, but he wondered where Bruce went every evening. Late one night, Dick went searching for a clue. He discovered a secret door that led to a flight of stairs. Dick followed the stairs down into the darkness.

He discovered an underground cavern filled with crime-fighting equipment. Dick couldn't believe his eyes. He was inside the Batcave! And there was the Batmobile. It could only mean one thing–Bruce Wayne was Batman!

Meanwhile across town, a gang of thugs had spotted a woman walking down the lonely streets of Gotham City.

"Easy money," the hoods sneered as they crept up alongside her. Then they snatched her purse and ran.

But an instant later a car came to a screeching halt in front of them. It was no ordinary car. It was the Batmobile!

"Oh, no!" one of the hoods screamed. "It's Batman!"

The hoodlums knew they were no match for Batman. But when the top of the Batmobile opened, they were surprised to see a young man!

"Look!" one of the crooks shouted. "That ain't Batman! It's just a kid! We can take *him* easy!"

But Dick quickly proved them wrong. He had spent years training as an acrobat. He leaped and dived about, kicking and punching the stunned thugs. In no time, he had knocked them all out.

"You'll be okay now," Dick told the woman. Then a hand grabbed him and tossed him into the Batmobile. It was Batman–and he was angry!

"Why can't we fight crime together?" Dick asked Batman as they drove back to Wayne Manor.

"You're too young," Batman answered. "Besides, Batman fights alone."

But Batman would soon need help. In another part of town a criminal genius called the Riddler was also plotting against him. While the Riddler had the brains to outwit the Batman, he didn't have the muscle to finish him off. The Riddler decided that Two-Face would make a perfect partner in crime.

The Riddler tracked down Two-Face and made an offer. Two-Face decided to flip a coin.

"If it comes up heads, we'll join forces," he explained. The coin hit the ground, landing heads up.

"Okay, partner, we have a deal," Two-Face said. "What's the plan?"

"Tomorrow night all of Gotham's richest people will be at a big party," the Riddler explained. "You'll crash the party and rob the guests! When Batman arrives to stop you, he'll walk right into our trap!"

The following night Two-Face arrived at the party right on schedule.

"All right, folks, this is an old-fashioned stickup," Two-Face growled at the terrified guests. His gang members were so busy robbing everyone, they didn't notice Bruce Wayne slip out of the room.

Moments later he returned . . . as Batman.

Two-Face smiled. "Begin Phase Two," he whispered to his gang. Then he ran out into the street and jumped into a nearby manhole. Batman followed him.

The manhole led into an abandoned subway tunnel. In the dim light Batman could see someone coming toward him. It was Two-Face carrying some kind of weapon!

"You thought you were on *my* trail," Two-Face snarled. "But it was all a trap." Two-Face pointed his weapon at Batman and fired!

Two-Face's weapon sent a fireball hurtling toward Batman.
Acting quickly, Batman pressed a button on his utility belt.
Instantly his costume was covered with a fireproof coating. The
ball of flame hit him full blast—but Batman was protected!

Meanwhile the explosive fireball shattered the tunnel walls. Stone and steel began to rain on Batman, and the ground beneath his feet collapsed. Batman felt himself sinking.

"I expect you'll be buried alive," Two-Face said as Batman sank deeper. "I'd love to stay and see you off, but crime's a-wastin' and I'm a very busy man!" Then Two-Face walked away.

Down, down Batman sank. "I'm finished," he thought. "There's no way to escape." But just before Batman's head disappeared below the sand, a green-gloved hand reached for him. With his last ounce of strength, Batman grabbed the hand. An instant later he felt himself being yanked up and out of the pit.

It was Dick! He had followed Batman!

Later Batman said, "I told you no crime fighting."

"Aren't you glad I didn't listen?" Dick answered. "I think it's time we became partners, since I just saved your life!"

"Okay," Batman said. "You've earned it. But what are we going to call you?"

Dick smiled. "My folks used to say I flew like a bird on the flying trapeze, so they called me Robin . . ."

"Batman and Robin," said Batman. "I like the sound of that!"

From then on, Batman and Robin would be partners, tracking down Two-Face, the Riddler, and every other criminal in Gotham City.